· ACTIVE MINDS ·

PHONICS FUN

My First Interactive Storybook

Publications International, Ltd.

Today is Bug's birthday. Cat makes buns and pancakes for breakfast. "Thank you for the treat," says Bug.

Bug plays with her friends. They go to the park. Bee sees a plane. A friend rides in the plane. Who is it?

Pig was in the plane. He visits Bug for her birthday.

"We will have fun," says Bug.

"Yippee!" say Cat and Bee.

Bug and her friends go to the fair. Pig plays a game. Bee eats lunch. Bug finds three balloons.

Bug and Pig run a race. "Go! Go! Go!" call Bee and Cricket. Bug runs fast. Pig runs slow. Bug wins the race.

After the race they swim in a pool.
The sun is hot. The water is cool.

fan

fun

pail

Bug's friends give her a party. Bug opens presents. Some gifts are big. Some gifts are small. Bug thanks her friends for her presents.

Bug likes music. Her friends like music, too. They play a song together.

Cat reads a book. The story has knights and swords. Cricket and Bee look at the pictures. Pig listens to the words.

s ee

r ead

ch air

Bug rests with her friends. "Birthdays are fun," says Bug. "Thank you for sharing the day with me."